The MESSED-UP MUSEUM

AN INTERACTIVE MYSTERY ADVENTURE

by Steve Brezenoff

illustrated by Marcos Calo

Field Trip Mysteries Adventures
are published by Stone Arch Books
a Capstone Imprint
1710 Roe Crest Drive
North Mankato, Minnesota 56003
www.mycapstone.com

Library of Congress Cataloging-in-Publication Data
is on file at the Library of Congress website.
978-1-4965-4859-7 (hardcover)
978-1-4965-4861-0 (paperback)
978-1-4965-4863-4 (eBook PDF)

Editor: Hank Musolf
Graphic Designer: Bobbie Nuytten
Production Artist: Laura Manthe

Summary: Follow Sam, Egg, Gum, and Cat as they try to solve the mystery
on their field trip to the film museum. When parts of a long-forgotten film
noir are missing, the junior detectives are on the case!

Printed in the United States of America.
PA66

YOU CHOOSE STORIES

A FIELD TRIP MYSTERIES ADVENTURE

The MESSED-UP MUSEUM

STONE ARCH BOOKS

a capstone imprint

Catalina Duran

A.K.A.: Cat

BIRTHDAY: February 15th

LEVEL: 6th Grade

INTERESTS:

Animals, being "green," field trips

Edward G. Garrison

A.K.A.: Egg

BIRTHDAY: May 14th

LEVEL: 6th Grade

INTERESTS:

Photography, field trips

James Shoo

A.K.A.: Gum

BIRTHDAY: November 19th

LEVEL: 6th Grade

INTERESTS:
Gum-chewing, field trips, and showing everyone what a crook Anton Gutman is

Samantha Archer

A.K.A.: Sam

BIRTHDAY: August 20th

LEVEL: 6th Grade

INTERESTS:
Old movies, field trips

FIELD TRIP 🚌 MYSTERIES

Samantha Archer has never been so excited for a field trip.

"For one thing," she says to her best friend Edward G. Garrison, better known to his friends as Egg, "the special exhibit for this trip is noir films of the 1940s and '50s, my favorites."

Egg and Sam, and their other two best friends Cat Duran and James "Gum" Shoo, spend every minute together—especially on field trips.

All four friends, along with the rest of Mr. Spade's sixth-grade class, are on the bus to the River City Museum of Moving Pictures. Today they'll see exhibits and learn about film noir, augmented and virtual reality, and "ancient" video games from the twentieth century.

"And another thing," Sam continued, "I'm most excited about the chaperone for this field trip."

TURN THE PAGE.

That's because today there's another person on the bus named Sam Archer: Samantha's grandfather, Samuel Archer.

Samantha lives with her grandparents, and she and her grandpa share a love of old mystery stories, TV shows, and movies.

"I couldn't miss this one," Grandpa Sam says, leaning around from the seat behind Sam and Egg. "They'll be screening a classic noir that I haven't seen since I was a young man."

"It's called The Long Sleep," says Sam. "They just discovered the film in some old vault in Hollywood."

The bus squeaks to a stop. "Here we are," calls out Mel the bus driver.

"I guess that's my cue," Grandpa Sam says. Grandpa Sam is supposed to help Mr. Spade lead the kids to the museum.

"See you inside!" says Sam.

Grandpa Sam hurries off the bus and through the revolving door into the museum.

"All right, everyone," Mr. Spade announces from the front. "In an orderly fashion, follow Mr. Archer into the front lobby."

The kids shuffle off the bus and inside, but Grandpa Sam is nowhere to be found.

"Now, where did he go?" Mr. Spade says.

Everyone looks at Sam.

"Maybe he had to go to the bathroom," she says.

"Hello, middle schoolers!" says a chipper man in a flamingo-colored suit. He is quite tall and thin, and he wears glasses that are tinted yellow. "I am Orlando, and I will be showing you around today."

All together, the class calls out, "Hi, Orlando."

He laughs and says, "Let's begin."

***

Their first stop is the display of classic video games.

"Now this is my kind of museum," Gum says. He stops to admire a game called *Fighting Force Five*.

TURN THE PAGE.

Orlando reaches over and taps the two-player button on the game. "I challenge you, young man!"

"You're on!" Gum says, stepping up to the game's huge cabinet.

As Gum and Orlando begin their game, Sam, Egg, and Cat look on. Egg snaps a few photos, but someone knocks into him.

"Hey!" Egg says.

Everyone turns.

Two men in green coveralls glare at them. Then they walk on to a machine in the corner labeled *Red, White, and Boom!* With some effort, they lift the machine up and turn it around. Their coveralls have "FunTime" stitched on the back.

Orlando leaves his game and hurries over to the men in green. "What are you doing?" he asks.

"The machine is in need of maintenance," one of them says. He hands Orlando a flimsy yellow sheet of paper.

Egg, Sam, and Cat hurry over for a closer listen.

"But I played it this morning," Orlando says. "I didn't notice any problems."

"Lots of problems," says the other man in green. "See? Look at the paper."

Both men turn away from Orlando and begin unscrewing the back panel of the arcade game's cabinet.

"Hmm," Orlando says. "Someone from engineering must have called them."

"But you said it isn't broken," Cat points out.

Orlando shakes his head, barely hearing her. He hands the paper to Sam and wanders off.

"Um, thanks?" Sam says. She looks at the paper and reads aloud, "'Electrical maintenance required by order of . . .' I can't make out the name."

"Well," Egg says, "if we want to get to the bottom of this, we'll have to speak to someone in engineering."

The repairmen, meanwhile, have hooked up a laptop to the back of the video game.

TURN THE PAGE.

"Class!" Mr. Spade says from the doorway. "Orlando would like us to move on now. You'll have plenty of free time to look around after the tour."

***

Their next stop is the augmented and virtual reality exhibit. Orlando slips a headset on Sam and powers up the computer.

Sam gasps.

"What's it like?" Cat asks eagerly.

"I'm on an alien planet," Sam says. "It's all red and dusty, like Mars, I guess?"

"Are there any aliens?" Gum asks.

"I don't know," Sam says. "Wait. I see a . . . dome city, way over there."

Orlando slips a controller into Sam's hand. "This will allow you to move to any point you can see. Look at where you want to go, and click the button."

"Whoa!" Sam shouts with glee. "I'm just outside the dome now. There are crazy-looking aliens everywhere!"

TURN THE PAGE.

Sam pulls off the goggles. "Let's check out the augmented reality now," she says to her three best friends.

The four friends follow Orlando.

"Right this way," he says as he leads them toward a door that reads "Augmented Reality, where fact and fantasy blend!"

"Step inside," Orlando says, pulling open the door.

Each takes a set of glasses—smaller than the VR headset—and slips them on as they go in. Orlando stays outside and closes the door.

It looks like a medieval castle dungeon inside: the walls are stone, and there are flickering torches on the wall.

A speaker somewhere plays sounds of wind whistling and water dripping.

"Wait!" Cat says, grabbing Sam's arm. "I saw something move over there."

She points frantically toward the far wall, where a door slowly opens.

"Let's go in," Sam says, pulling Cat along.

Beyond the door is a long, dark hallway, barely lit by more torches. Someone is at the far end.

"Who is that?" Egg says, squinting through his regular glasses and the AR glasses.

Suddenly the lights become brighter. It's a seven-foot-tall ogre wielding a big stone club.

"Arrrr!" it roars at them.

The four friends scream and run back into the first room, but there they find a scary trio of cruel-looking trolls.

"What's going on?!" Cat screams.

"Look at your hands," Orlando tells them over the speakers. "Use your magic!"

The four friends find their hands are glowing, one hand in blue and the other in red.

"Blast them!" Gum shouts. He raises his blue hand and motions toward the group of trolls. Ice power streams from his fingers. The trolls are frozen in place.

TURN THE PAGE.

"Whoa," Cat says. "I get it now."

She raises her red hand toward the charging ogre. Flames blast from her hand. The ogre screams and turns to dust.

"Well done," Orlando says, opening the door. "You can play again during your free time. Come on out."

"That was amazing," Sam says as they leave. "I hope I can zap something next time."

"Me too," Egg says. "I just wish I could take photos, but I don't suppose that would work."

Orlando laughs. "No, but we do sell photos of the experience in our gift shop," he says.

"Wait a second," Cat says as they head out of the VR/AR exhibit. She rubs her left wrist with her right hand. "My silver bracelet is gone."

"Bracelet?" Gum says.

"She wears it practically every day," Egg says. "She got it from sponsoring those seals at the zoo last year."

"Ohhh," Gum says, pretending to remember. "That bracelet."

"It must have fallen off in the AR room," Sam says. "You did blast that ogre pretty hard."

"Let's go back and look," Gum says. "The tour can wait if Cat's upset."

"Our staff is very thorough," Orlando says, having overheard the problem. "I have already let them know. If it turns up, I'll let you know."

"Oh," Cat says, sounding a little disappointed. "OK. Thanks."

***

The next and last stop is the film noir exhibit.

"Grandpa Sam!" Sam says, hurrying toward the exhibit. Her friends follow. "There you are!"

"There *you* are," Grandpa Sam says. "I've been waiting here for the class to show up."

"Here we are?" Sam says. "Grandpa, you were supposed to wait for us in the lobby. You missed most of the tour!"

TURN THE PAGE.

"Oh, I'm sorry about that," he says, "The truth is I went to find a bathroom."

"I knew it," Sam says.

"But then I saw someone I thought I knew," he says, "a very long time ago."

"And?" Egg says, expecting a story.

"I tried to find her in this place, but it's such a maze." Grandpa Sam says.

"The official tour ends with one more stop," Orlando says. "But first, who likes popcorn?"

The whole class cheers.

***

Everyone gets a small box of popcorn, and they're led into the theater. Sam and her friends sit with her Grandpa near the front.

"Did you know," Grandpa Sam says as the lights go down and the opening credits begin, "I know someone in this movie?"

"An actor?" Sam says.

"That is so cool," Cat adds.

"In fact," Grandpa says, "she was my sweetheart."

Sam is shocked. "Before Grandma?" she asks.

"Of course!" Grandpa Sam says. "Once I met your grandmother, there was never another girl for me."

***

The movie was ninety minutes long. Toward the end, though, just after the suspenseful climax and the mystery's reveal, the screen goes blank for a few seconds. Then up pops the old-timey "THE END."

"That was a weird ending," Sam says. "So which actor did you know?"

Grandpa Sam is stumped. "None of them," he says. "But I could have sworn Jasmine de la Fleur was in this movie. It was her only movie."

The lights come up. As they leave the theater, Egg says, "It looked like some frames were missing at the end. Maybe that was her scene."

"Maybe," Grandpa says, looking across the room.

TURN THE PAGE.

Sam follows his gaze. He's watching a woman about his age wearing a flat, round cap.

"Well, my goodness," Grandpa Sam says. He takes off his hat and puts it on his chest. "That's her. That's Jasmine de la Fleur."

But as quickly as he spotted her, she hurries away. The four friends and Grandpa Sam hurry after her, but she vanishes through a door marked "Authorized Personnel Only."

"And that concludes the tour," Orlando announces. "We apologize for the technical difficulties at the end of the film. Now please enjoy your free time at the museum. Have fun!"

"So what should we do with our free time?" Gum says. He pulls out a pack of kiwi-strawberry flavored gum and pops a piece.

"Isn't it obvious?" Sam says. "We have a mystery to solve."

"Yes, but which one?" Egg says.

TO SOLVE THE MYSTERY OF THE VIDEO GAME THAT'S NOT BROKEN, CONTINUE ON TO PAGE 21.

TO SOLVE THE MYSTERY OF THE MISSING MOVIE FRAMES, TURN TO PAGE 52.

TO SOLVE THE MYSTERY OF THE MISSING BRACELET, TURN TO PAGE 79.

"I was hoping we'd choose this mystery," Gum says, stepping up to *Fighting Force Five*. "Someone find Orlando so we can finish that grudge match!"

"Gum," Sam says, "we're not here to play games." She takes the yellow paper from her back pocket and unfolds it.

"Yeah," Cat says, looking over Sam's shoulder at the paper. "We're to investigate games."

"One game," Egg says. He snaps a few photos of the men working on the back of *Red, White, and Boom!*

"Let's get started then," Sam says.

The sleuths walk toward the game and the two workers in green coveralls.

Cat smiles at the men. "Sorry to bother you," she says. "We were just wondering what's wrong with this game."

"Yeah," Gum says. "I want to give it a try. Looks fun."

TURN THE PAGE.

"It's not fun," says the man in green coveralls with the busted-looking nose. He stands up. "It's a boring game. Now bug off."

"All right, all right," Sam says.

The four friends move out of earshot. "They're not on the level," Sam says.

"You think they're up to something?" Egg says.

Sam nods. "Time to get to work," she says.

"Let's talk to Orlando and see what he knows," Egg says.

"Excuse us," Cat says as she walks up to Orlando, who is clearly distracted.

"Orlando!" Gum says in a booming voice.

The tour guide snaps out of his daydream. "Oh, hi!" he says, suddenly smiling. "You kids lost?"

"No," Sam says. "But you might be."

"What?" Orlando says.

"That video game that's being repaired," Sam explains. "You didn't know there was anything wrong with it, right?"

"That's right," Orlando says. "But I have to go. Excuse me."

"Before you go, can you read this name?" Egg asks. "You must know everyone in engineering, right?"

Sam hands over the yellow paper.

Orlando squints at the paper. "It ought to say Thurman's name. Or maybe Kelly, his assistant. But this? Just looks like a scribble."

Orlando folds the paper, slips it into the pocket of his jacket, and walks off.

"That was a dead end," Gum says.

"Not at all," Sam says. "We just got two leads: Thurman and Kelly."

"Then I guess we head down to engineering," Cat says.

"If we can even get in," Sam says. "It's probably employees only."

"Maybe we should call the video game company," Egg says, pulling out his cell phone.

To go to Engineering, turn to page 24.
To call the video game company, turn to page 41.

"How will we find it?" Cat asks.

"Let's check the basement," Sam says. "That's where they usually put stuff like that in museums."

Gum nods. "This way," he says, pointing toward a sign for the stairway.

Egg pulls open the door for his friends. Grandpa Sam is in the stairway, heading out.

"Where are you kids going?" he says. "I don't think you're supposed to go downstairs."

His granddaughter crosses her arms. "What were you doing down there, Grandpa?" she asks.

"Grandpa stuff!" he says. "Mind your own business, and follow the rules. I don't think your teacher would like it if you kids were wandering where you're not supposed to wander."

"Grandpa," Sam says. "Do you know why we want to go to the basement?"

"Why don't you tell me?" Grandpa Sam replies.

She grins at him.

TURN THE PAGE.

"A couple of mooks are in the video game exhibit right now," Sam says. "I don't think they're on the level. We gave a third and they threw me bunk."

"That right?" Grandpa says. "Couple of hoods, huh? Do we drop a dime, or give 'em the bum's rush?"

"Um, Sam Archers?" Gum says, looking back and forth between Sam and her grandfather. "What are you two talking about?"

Grandpa puts an arm around Sam's shoulders. "My moll here just gave me the skinny on your case, snoopers," he says.

Sam's three friends' eyes go wide. "Wait," Gum finally says. "I might have missed a few words there, but does that mean you don't mind us trying to solve a mystery?"

"Mind?" Grandpa says. "I'm a shamus at heart. Where do you think the moll gets it from?"

"I'll take that to mean he wants to help," Cat says, looking at Sam.

Sam nods. "Come on," she says.

***

"There it is," Sam says. A black plaque next to an open door reads "Engineering—Authorized Personnel Only."

"Do we just walk in?" Cat says.

"Door's open," Gum says. "Why not?"

With that, he strolls into the open doorway. His friends and Grandpa Sam hurry after him.

A young woman sits at a cluttered, metal desk in a small office. There are no windows, and one door on each wall to the left and right.

The right door is open, and seems to lead to a storage room. The left is closed, but there's a light on beyond it and shining under the door.

"Err," the woman says. "Can I help you?"

She wears loose-fitting jeans and a denim shirt, stained with grease.

"I think you wandered off the tour," the woman says. "That door should really be closed."

TURN THE PAGE.

"We're not lost," Sam says. "We're looking for Thurman."

The woman looks at Grandpa Sam, as if to say, *What is this all about?*

"You heard the girl," he says. "May we speak to Thurman, please?"

"Um," the woman says. "Just a second."

She opens the closed door and sticks her head inside.

"What is it, Kelly?" booms a man's voice from the other room.

"There are some kids and an old man here to see you," Kelly replies. "I think."

"Kids and an old man . . . ," Thurman says. "I don't have any appointments today. Tell them to go away."

Kelly closes the door. "You heard him," she says. "Now, unless there's something I can do for you, please head back to the exhibits upstairs."

To question Kelly, continue on to page 29.
To rush into Thurman's office anyway, turn to page 37.

"Actually," Sam says as she walks to Kelly's desk, "there is something you can help us with."

Sam leans both palms on the woman's desk and looks down at her.

"OK," Kelly says. She sits farther back in her chair as if trying to escape Sam's glare.

"It seems," says Grandpa, "that two suspicious men are working on a video game without authorization."

"What makes you think they don't have authorization?" Kelly asks. "If they're here working, they came in through the service entrance."

"So?" Sam says.

"So," Kelly says, "that means they had to present paperwork—a work order—to me or Thurman . . . or Maddy around back, I suppose."

"Who's Maddy?" Sam asks.

TURN THE PAGE.

Kelly looks from one young detective to the other and finally at Grandpa Sam. "Who did you people say you were again?" she asks.

"We're investigators," Gum says.

"Amateur investigators," Cat says in a quiet voice.

"I see," Kelly says. "Well, since Thurman won't see you and I've had enough of you, why don't you five just get out of here."

"Fine, fine," Grandpa says. He takes his granddaughter by the hand and leads her and her friends out. "No need to be rude."

Kelly closes the door behind them. Across the hall from her office is a sign pointing left. It reads "Loading Bay in Rear."

"Huh," Egg says as he takes a photo of the sign. "You don't suppose 'Maddy around back' works in the loading bay, do you?"

TO HEAD BACK UPSTAIRS, CONTINUE ON TO PAGE 31.
TO TRACK DOWN MADDY, TURN TO PAGE 33.

But Grandpa Sam says, "Sorry, kids. I suppose not every case can be cracked. Have you spent any time in the VR/AR exhibit yet? I was just thinking—"

"Grandpa!" Sam says suddenly as the five of them start back upstairs. "We don't give up just like that. We have so many more options!"

"We do?" Gum says as they reach the main floor.

Grandpa Sam opens the door. Mr. Spade is standing right there.

"Ahem," Mr. Spade says. "Like grandpa, like granddaughter, hmm?"

"Oh, Mr. Spade," Grandpa Sam says. "I was just showing these fine children to the restroom and we got lost. This crazy place is a maze, I'll tell you."

"Is that right?" Mr. Spade says, eying Sam, Gum, Egg, and Cat.

They all nod in agreement with Grandpa's lie, except Cat, who looks like she's about to burst.

TURN THE PAGE.

"Ahh!" she finally says. "We weren't looking for the bathroom, Mr. Spade. We were looking for the head engineer's office."

"Why?" Mr. Spade asks.

"We were," Cat says, looking at her feet, "investigating."

"Another mystery," Mr. Spade says. "I'm sorry about this, kids. And you too, Mr. Archer. But I've spoken to these four about this very issue dozens if not hundreds of times."

"Thirty-six times, Mr. Spade," Gum says.

"Fine, thirty-six," Mr. Spade says. Then he adds under his breath, "Wow, we go on a lot of field trips."

The five amateur detectives nod.

"Anyway, it's back on the bus for you," Mr. Spade says. "You'll miss the rest of the field trip."

THE END

TO FOLLOW ANOTHER PATH, TURN TO PAGE 20.

The kids follow the sign to the left. It winds through the belly of the museum, climbing slowly as it goes. Finally the hallway ends at an open doorway.

"That must be the loading bay," Grandpa Sam says.

Beyond the doorway is a cement platform. Then it drops off to a wide, grease-stained paved area. Two huge garage doors are open to the outside and a quiet back alley.

A green delivery van is parked in the loading bay with its rear to the platform. Its back doors are open, like it's dropping something off or picking something up.

The five amateur sleuths walk through the doorway.

"Whoa, whoa," says a man as he walks next to the van. He was hidden just past the corner of the vehicle's open back doors, so they didn't see him until they stepped outside. He wears an olive green jumpsuit with a shirt underneath. The jumpsuit is a little too small for him.

TURN THE PAGE.

A tag pinned to his shirt reads *Arnold*.

"This exit is not for use by, uh, museum guests," Arnold says. "Staff only."

"We're looking for a woman who works here," Egg says. "Kelly sent us."

"Kelly?" Arnold says. "In engineering?" His cheeks turn red.

"That's her," Sam says. "Good friend of ours. Think you can help us?"

"Well, gosh," Arnold says. "If you're friends of Kelly, sure I'll help. She's great, isn't she?"

"Oh, the best," Gum says.

"Sorry to say, though," Arnold says. "No women work back here. Just me, Arnold Madison."

"But she specifically said we should talk to Maddy," Sam says. "And—oh."

"I'm Maddy," he says. "It's short for Madison."

"Sorry," Egg says. "We just figured . . . sorry."

"Well," Maddy says. "What can I do to help Kelly—I mean, and to help you, of course."

TURN THE PAGE.

"There are a couple of men working on *Red, White, and Boom!* today," Gum says. "We don't think they have authorization."

"Oh, they sure do," Maddy says. "I checked the work order myself. All in order."

"And who called in for the service?" Sam asks.

"Must've been Kelly or Thurm," Maddy says.

"Alright," Grandpa says. "Thanks for your time."

The five sleuths head back down the hall, past the engineering office, and up the stairs. They run into Mr. Spade in the main corridor.

"There you five are," he says. "Time to get back on the bus."

"Already?" Egg says. "But we haven't solved the mystery . . . er, mystery game in the AR room."

"Sorry!" Mr. Spade says. "Time's up."

THE END

To follow another path, turn to page 20.

"Hey, what's that?" Gum says, pointing over Kelly's head.

She turns around. "What's what?" she says.

"Now!" Gum shouts, and the five amateur detectives rush through Thurman's door and slam it behind them.

"What is the meaning of this?" Thurman says as he stands up from his worktable. He's a huge man in blue overalls and a very greasy white shirt with a collar. "Kelly!"

"We're sorry to barge in like this," Grandpa Sam says. "But these kids really need to speak to you. It's urgent."

Thurman considers them. His brow is furrowed. His thick mustache flutters, and the muscles in his arms seem ready to burst through the fabric of his shirt.

"Urgent?" he says. He seems to calm down. "Fine."

Kelly puts her head in the door. "Sorry, Thurm," she says. "I tried to make them leave."

TURN THE PAGE.

"It's fine," Thurman says. "What's this all about?"

"Well, sir," Cat says, "we saw a couple of men working on a video game."

"*Red, White, and Boom!*" Gum adds.

"All right," Thurman says. "We have specialists in to work on the games all the time. Some of the technology is very game specific, and Kelly and I wouldn't know what to do."

"I don't think we put in a repair order for that game, Thurm," Kelly says. She leans on the wall just inside the door to Thurman's office.

"That's odd," he says. He walks across the office in one huge stride and pulls open a filing cabinet. "Let's see. . . . Ah, here it is."

He pulls out a folder.

"Now, *Red, White, and Boom!* came in four months ago. We had some wiring issues at the time, but I think Kelly handled that."

Kelly nods. "I had some help over the phone," she says. "But it was pretty simple."

"Well, there you have it," Thurman says. "There shouldn't be anyone working on that machine today. If anyone called for repairs, it would be us. And we didn't."

"We'd better get back up there, then," Cat says. "Who knows what those men might be up to!"

***

The four friends, Grandpa Sam, and Thurman hurry upstairs to the video game exhibit. "Where are they?" Thurman says, huffing and puffing with fury.

"They're gone!" Sam says, rushing to the game cabinet. "They were right here, working."

Thurman stomps to the machine. He looks over the back panel. He presses the button for a single player game. The game starts correctly, with an eight-bit melody and everything.

"Seems OK to me," he says. "Why don't you kids play a few games? If anything seems wrong, let me know. You know where to find me."

TURN THE PAGE.

With that, the huge man waddles off.

"Kids," Grandpa Sam says, "I don't know how to say this, but that was . . ."

"A huge waste of time?" Sam says. "The criminals are gone, and now that guy thinks we're off our heads."

Grandpa nods.

"If they even were criminals," Cat says. "Sounds like it was just a paperwork mix-up."

"There you kids are," Mr. Spade says as he steps into the video game exhibit. "Time to head back to school."

"Already?" Egg says.

"Meet in front, please," Mr. Spade says. "You too, Mr. Archer."

"Boy," Gum says as he chews sadly, "I never thought a field trip to a video game museum would be so boring."

THE END

TO FOLLOW ANOTHER PATH, TURN TO PAGE 20.

Egg quickly dials the number. After a moment he says, "Hello?" He whispers so he won't disturb anyone in the museum.

He and his friends are in the corner of the video game exhibit. Across the room, the men in green are still fiddling with the back of the machine.

"This is FunTime Classic Amusement," says a man's voice. "Can I help you?"

"Um, yes," says Egg, doing his best impression of an adult. It isn't very good. "I'm calling from the Museum of Moving Pictures."

"Oh, hi," the man replies. "How's the exhibit going?"

"Oh, fine," Egg says. "Of course, we are having that problem with the *Red, White, and Boom!* machine."

"Problem?" the man says. "There was a wiring issue, but I thought your engineer Kelly Reinhart took care of that."

TURN THE PAGE.

"Oh, yes," Egg says. He coughs as his voice cracks. "I mean, yes. When was that again?"

"Look, who is this?" the man says.

"I'll ask the questions here!" Egg barks into the phone.

"All right, all right, calm down," the man says. "Boy, am I having a weird day. First two of our uniforms go missing, and now this. So what's the problem with the machine now?"

"Did you say two uniforms went missing?" Egg says.

Sam gasps. Cat covers her mouth. Gum, who hasn't been paying attention at all, announces, "Hey, guys! I have the high score on *Alien Blastazoid Three-thousand*!"

"Yeah, why?" the man says. "Not exactly the crime of the century. Now, what's the serial number on that machine again? I'll look it up."

"Hold on," Egg says. He covers the phone. "He wants the serial number."

"So give it to him," Sam says.

"How?" Egg asks.

Sam grabs the phone from him, marches across the room, and sits down next to the repairmen. They are in the process of replacing the back panel.

"What do you want?" the grumpier one says.

"Where's the serial number?" Sam asks.

"Why?" says the less grumpy one.

"No reason," Sam says.

"It's right there," says the grumpy one with the broken-looking nose.

Sam leans closer and reads aloud in a very deep voice, making sure the phone is near her face but out of sight of the repairmen, "The serial number is One-H-three-four-seven-dash-A-six."

"Now scram," the grumpy one says.

"OK," Sam says. "Bye!"

She hurries back and hands Egg the phone.

"Why are you like that?" Cat asks in whisper.

TURN THE PAGE.

Sam looks at her, confused. "Like what?" she asks.

"Brave," Cat says.

Sam gives her a half hug. "Search me," she says.

"That's not your machine," the man on the phone says. "Check it again. Last digit is six, not nine?"

"Right, it's definitely a six," Egg says.

"Well this is a fine how-do-you-do," the man says. "Looks like we shipped you the wrong machine. Yours is with a firm called Acme Enterprise, and you have theirs."

"What's the difference?" Egg asks. "Same machine, right?"

"The one you have right now is a little newer," the man says. "So the one Acme has is a bit older. Earlier production model, all that. I can have them switched if you like."

"Which is more valuable?" Egg asks.

Turn the page.

"Oh, the older one," the man says. "For sure. That year is quite rare. First year they made them."

"Oh, I have to go," Egg says. He hangs up.

"Why'd you do that?" Sam asks. "We're so close to having this solved!"

"I think I might have it solved already," Egg says. "I think they're spies."

"It's what we've always dreamed of," Sam says with a wistful look on her face.

"Acme has the museum's game," Egg says. "It's more valuable, so they should want to keep it."

"Yeah?" Gum says. "These guys aren't wearing Acme uniforms."

"Right," Egg says. "They're wearing uniforms that were stolen from FunTime this morning."

"Ah," Gum says. "Go on."

"This morning, we saw them try to download information to a laptop," Egg says.

"Maybe that's just normal repair stuff," Sam says.

"Maybe," Egg says. "But remember no one here at the museum ordered any repairs. Orlando said so, and the man on the phone said so."

"But if they're from Acme," Cat says slowly, "why pretend to be from FunTime? It's their machine anyway."

"Because Acme doesn't exist," Sam says. "It's a front."

"A front?" Gum asks.

"A fake company to hide some kind of criminal activity," Sam says.

"In this case, espionage," Egg says.

"That means spying," Sam explains.

"We know," Cat and Gum say.

The four friends stand and stare at the men in green. Soon, they both grab hold of the machine and lift it onto a dolly.

"They're taking it!" Sam says. "What do we do?"

To try to stop them, turn to page 48.
To get some help, turn to page 50.

Sam runs over to block the workers in green.

"All right, that's it," says the grumpy man in green. He grabs Sam by the arms and lifts her off the ground.

"What do you think you're doing?!" Mr. Spade shouts as he comes into the exhibit. "Let go of that girl this instant!"

The man sets her down. Sam and her friends run to Mr. Spade.

"Let's get out of here," the less grumpy man in green says.

Three security guards burst in and stop them. "We heard shouting," says one. "Where are you two taking that machine?"

The man and his partner push the dolly but go a little too fast. The video game topples off the dolly and crashes to the ground.

Sam picks up a scrap of plastic.

"Hey, look at this," Sam says. "This was taped to the inside of the cabinet."

"It's a floppy disk!" Egg says. "Information technology almost as old as this game."

"We failed," says one of the men. "The information is theirs. They'll turn it over to their government. All is lost."

"All right, all right," the security guard says. "The police are on their way."

The four sleuths stand together in the hall a few moments later. The exhibit is closed off so the mess could be cleaned up.

"Hello, kids," says Grandpa Sam. "I heard a commotion. Anything exciting?"

"Nah," Sam says. "Just international spies, smuggled computer disks, and exploding video games."

"Ah," Grandpa says. "Normal field trip then."

THE END

TO FOLLOW ANOTHER PATH, TURN TO PAGE 20.

"Guards!" Sam shouts. "Guards!"

"Just keep going," says one of the men in green to the other.

But as they push the dolly into the corridor, two security guards appear and block their path.

"Someone need some help?" says one of the guards.

"No, officers," says one of the men in green. "We have authorization to remove this game."

"That's right, Johnny," says Orlando as he walks up. "I heard some shouting, though. Is everything OK?"

Sam, Egg, Cat, and Gum run up to Orlando. "Everything is not OK!" Egg says.

"These men are spies," Sam adds.

"International spies," Gum says.

"Probably," Cat says.

The three men look at the four young detectives. For a moment, no one speaks.

Then all three men begin laughing.

"It's true!" Egg says. "They're not really from FunTime!"

"Those uniforms are stolen!" Sam insists.

"Kids these days," says one of the men in green.

"I am still not sure who called you," Orlando says. "You're here to bring in a replacement unit, right?"

"Yup, it's in the van," the man in green replies.

With that, they push the dolly through the front door.

Orlando strolls away, looking less concerned about the men in green.

"Well," Gum says, "we tried."

"Not hard enough," Sam says, sulking.

"There you kids are," Mr. Spade says. "Time to go. I'm gathering your classmates now."

THE END

TO FOLLOW ANOTHER PATH, TURN TO PAGE 20.

The sleuths wander for a bit outside of the film noir exhibit.

He and the four young friends sit down together on the red benches that line the walls of the theater lobby.

All around are posters of noir film stars, cool-looking detectives, scary-looking hoods, women in glamorous dresses.

Orlando the tour guide passes by.

"Can you help us with something?" Sam says, standing as he passes.

"Oh, of course," Orlando says. He seems a little distracted.

"We saw a woman my grandpa knows go into that door," she says, pointing at the authorized personnel only door. "Does she work here?"

"I assume so, if she went in there," Orlando says. "What's her name?"

"Jasmine de la Fleur," Grandpa Sam says.

Orlando shakes his head. "Nope," he says. "No one works here by that name. Must have been someone else."

"I'm sure you're right," Grandpa Sam says. "I haven't seen her in ages, after all. My mistake."

Orlando smiles and walks off.

"He's lying," Grandpa Sam says. His voice is serious.

"Oh, Grandpa," Sam says. "Why would he lie?"

"I don't know, but we should find out why," Grandpa says. "Let's follow him."

"I guess he's where Sam gets it from," Gum says, laughing.

Orlando wanders throughout the museum. He stops sometimes to speak to a guest or help another student from Mr. Spade's class.

"This is getting us nowhere," Sam says. She takes her grandpa's hand. "I don't think this guy is a strong lead, Grandpa."

"Maybe you're right," he admits. "I just couldn't sit there and do nothing."

TURN THE PAGE.

"I don't get it," Gum says. "Aren't we trying to find out who cut the last scene out of the movie? What does this woman have to do with that?"

"She was in the missing scene," Egg says. "Right, Mr. Archer?"

"I think so, anyway," he says.

"Well, Orlando might know something too," Gum says. "He works here."

"So what?" Cat says. "Should we just stroll up to him and ask?" She laughs.

"All right," Gum says. And off he goes.

"Hey, Orlando," Gum says.

The man in the pink suit turns, startled. "Oh, hello," he says.

"What happened to the last scene of the movie?" Gum asks.

"Ah," Orlando says. "That's on my mind as well. The film should be complete. I've been looking for our projectionist, Sebastian, but he appears to be on a break."

TURN THE PAGE.

Sam pulls out her notepad and writes down "Sebastian—projectionist."

"Does he take a lot of breaks?" Sam asks.

Orlando shrugs. "Projectionists are rare these days," he says. "And he's been doing the job for fifty years. Nowadays he gets whatever he wants."

"Anyone else who might know anything?" Sam asks.

Orlando sighs. "I suppose I'll speak to the woman who is guest curator of the exhibit," he says. "She's so odd, though."

"What's her name?" Sam asks.

"Her name is Rouge Poisson," he says. "Now I really must go." With that, he hurries away.

"I guess we have two leads now," Cat says.

"And two suspects," Sam adds as she closes her notebook.

"I don't care about that," Grandpa says. "I want to find Jasmine."

TO TRY TO FIND JASMINE, TURN THE PAGE.
TO SPEAK TO SEBASTIAN, TURN TO PAGE 60.

The four friends and Grandpa Sam return to the film noir exhibit. It's pretty quiet.

"Looks like everyone is checking out the video games or the VR," Egg says.

"Wish I was!" Gum says.

Grandpa looks around the exhibit casually. "Excuse me a moment, kids," he says. "I'll be back in a bit."

They watch him walk off. On the far side of the exhibit, he stops to talk to a woman in an old-fashioned outfit.

"She looks like she might have stepped off the screen during a *black and white* movie," Cat says a little wistfully, "except she's in color."

"Come on," Egg says. "Let's get to work. There's an info desk."

"But there's no one there," Sam points out.

They walk over to the desk. A little paper card is folded there so it will stand up. It says "Back in fifteen minutes."

"Fifteen minutes from when?" Egg says.

Turn the page.

"From when they left the note," Gum says, "obviously."

"Which was when?" Egg says.

"Fifteen minutes before they get back," Gum says, "obviously."

Egg sighs. He leans on the counter, and together they wait.

After an hour, Egg rolls his head, sore from waiting. "It's definitely been more than fifteen minutes," he says.

Mr. Spade strolls into the noir exhibit. "Ah!" he says. "I had a feeling I'd find Sam Archer and her detective agency here. Time to go, kids. Group up in the lobby."

He walks off, and just then Grandpa Sam turns up again.

"There you are," Sam says. "You've been gone for ages. It's time to get on the bus."

Grandpa smiles. "Sounds lovely," he says.

"Not to me," Sam says. "We didn't solve the mystery."

"I solved my mystery," Grandpa Sam says. "That was Jasmine de la Fleur. And I just spent an hour with her in the coffee shop catching up. It's been fifty years."

"That was her?" Sam says.

"She's lovely," Cat adds.

"I wish I'd gotten to meet her," Sam says.

"Oh, you will," Grandpa says. "She's coming over for dinner tomorrow night. Which reminds me. I'd better call your grandma to warn her."

THE END

TO FOLLOW ANOTHER PATH, TURN TO PAGE 20.

"If Orlando can't find Sebastian," Grandpa points out, "how will we?"

"Orlando is just wandering around," Sam says, "and he's already giving up."

The four friends and Grandpa Sam walk up to the information booth in the front lobby.

"Can I help you?" asks the woman at the desk.

"We're looking for Sebastian, the projectionist," Sam says. "Have you seen him?"

"Yes, in fact," she says. "He just came in with a white package. I think it was a sandwich."

"Where did he go?" Egg asks.

"He probably eats in the break room," the woman says.

"Of course," Sam says with a smile. "Thanks!"

They hurry away. "Now we have to find the break room," Gum says. "It could be anywhere."

"And it's definitely off-limits to us," Cat points out.

"Bah!" Grandpa Sam says. "You can get away with a lot when you're my age. Come on."

Grandpa Sam leads them down the main hall until they reach a guard in a blue uniform. "Young fellow," Grandpa says, "would you mind pointing me to the employee break room?"

"The break room?" the guard says. He looks over the four kids. "What for?"

"Oh, it's my brother, Sebastian," Grandpa says. He reaches into his pocket and pulls out a wallet. "He left home without it. Again!"

The guard smiles gently. "All right," he says. "It's just down this hallway to the end. Swing a right, and it's just past the restrooms."

"Thanks, officer," Grandpa Sam says.

The five amateur detectives hurry along.

"I'm impressed, Grandpa," Sam says. "You should hang out with us more often."

"Here it is," Cat says. "We should knock."

Gum barrels right past her and opens the door.

TURN THE PAGE.

A man Grandpa's age sits at the table in the middle of the room with a sandwich at his mouth. "Can I help you?" he asks.

"You must be Sebastian," Grandpa says. "Mind if I sit? I've been on my feet all morning."

"Course not," Sebastian says.

The four friends shuffle in and close the door.

"You showed the movie this morning, right?" says Egg.

Sebastian nods. "I show every movie at the noir exhibit, if that's what you mean," he says. "You think showing a movie that old with a projector is as easy as picking up a remote and pushing play?"

Grandpa laughs. "I hear that!" he says.

"So what happened at the end?" Sam asks.

"Oh, you noticed that, huh?" Sebastian says. "Real shame. When I came in this morning to set up the reels for the film, I noticed someone had been there right away. Found an empty coffee cup. I never leave my trash around the booth."

TURN THE PAGE.

Sam notes in her book "empty coffee cup."

"Anyway," Sebastian goes on, "one of the cans—that is, the cases the films are kept in—had been opened. Old films are split into reels that need to be threaded into the projector so the movie can play. Each reel has a filmstrip in it, and you can see each frame of the movie if you hold it up to light. When I threaded the third reel, the last one, it was obvious what someone had done when I looked at the frames toward the end. A messy bit of editing, to say the least."

"But you showed the film anyway?" Egg asks.

Sebastian shrugs. "Sure," he says. "What choice did I have? Probably should have mentioned it to Orlando, but it was almost show time."

"So you have no idea who did this?" Grandpa asks.

Sebastian shakes his head as he chews a bite of his sandwich. "Sorry," he says. "Someone who drinks coffee out of cardboard cups, I guess."

The five amateur detectives leave the break room.

"Great," Grandpa says. "That doesn't narrow it down at all."

"So now what?" Cat says. "Is this a dead end?"

"No way," Sam says. She takes out her notebook. "Coffee in a cardboard cup and access to the projection booth before Sebastian came in this morning, or after he left last night."

"That's not all," Grandpa Sam says. "Whoever it was knew enough about old movies to find the third reel and cut off just the right bit of film and tape it together again."

"Even if it was messy," Egg pointed out.

"So who would know about old movies?" Sam asks.

"That guest curator, Rouge Poisson," Cat says. "If she's so close to the exhibit, she might be just the person we need to talk to."

To wait at the noir exhibit for Rouge Poisson, turn to page 66.
To search the rest of the museum for Rouge Poisson, turn to page 71.

"I feel like I should be doing something," Grandpa says.

For the last thirty minutes, Grandpa and the kids have been sitting and waiting, and watching that door marked "authorized personnel only."

"She has to turn up eventually," Cat says. "She's the guest curator."

"Oh, I don't care about her," Grandpa says. "I'm waiting for Jasmine."

"Oh," Cat says. "Well, she went in there. She'll probably come out, right?"

"Unless there's another door she can use," Gum points out.

A few minutes later, someone steps up to the bench from the other side.

"I suppose you'll stay here all day until I appear, hmm?" says a woman's voice.

They all look up. She's Grandpa's age and quite tall. Her hair is shaped in an old-fashioned style, and a veil hangs down from her red, flat-topped hat.

"Are you Rouge Poisson?" Egg asks.

"Yes," the woman says. "I am."

Grandpa stands. "Forgive me," he says. "I took you to be Jasmine de la Fleur, the actress in *The Long Sleep*."

She pulls back her veil and smiles at Grandpa Sam. "Hello, Samuel," she says. "I'm happy to see you, and I am Jasmine de la Fleur."

"But you said you were Rouge Poisson!" Sam says.

"And I am," she insists. "That is the name I use today. But once I was Jasmine de la Fleur— when I was much younger, when I struggled as an actress."

Grandpa Sam blushes and holds his hat to his chest. "Then you do remember me," he says.

"Of course," she says. "I'm sorry for running from you earlier. I was caught off guard."

The two gaze into each other's eyes for a long moment until Samantha gives her grandpa a little shove.

TURN THE PAGE.

"Earth to Grandpa," she says. "Remember Grandma?"

"Oh, sorry," he stammers.

"I heard you married Brigid O'Shaughnessy," Jasmine says. She looks at Samantha. "You have your grandma's face."

Sam smiles. "She's a beautiful lady," she says.

"That she is," Jasmine says. "But you children have been looking for me?"

"Finally," Gum says, "Did you cut from the movie thing or what?"

"Did I what?" she says.

"It seems someone has removed the last few moments of *The Long Sleep*," Grandpa explains. "Your scene is gone from the film they're showing here."

She gasps lightly and covers her mouth. "Why wasn't I told?" she says. "I'm the guest curator. Where is Orlando?"

"Then it wasn't you," Grandpa says.

TURN THE PAGE.

"But who does that leave as a suspect?" Sam says.

"Why, Samuel," Jasmine says, smiling. "Did you snip a few frames so you could have a little souvenir of the good old days?"

"I certainly did not," Grandpa says.

Jasmine pouts at him. "Ah, well," she says. "We'll always have Paris."

"You went to Paris together?" Cat says.

"It's just an expression, kid," Grandpa Sam says.

Mr. Spade strolls into the noir exhibit. "Hey, folks," he says. "Time to skedaddle. On the bus!"

"We're out of time," Egg says.

"And the mystery remains unsolved," Sam says.

"Says you," Grandpa says. "Jasmine and I solved our mystery."

THE END

To follow another path, turn to page 20.

The four friends and Grandpa Sam spend the next hour and a half searching the museum.

"Excuse us," Grandpa Sam says as he and the kids walk up to the information booth. "Where can I find Ms. Poisson?"

"She should be around here somewhere," said the young man behind the counter. "She's usually wandering the exhibit as if she's a guest."

"Is it all hers?" Cat asks.

The young man nods and says, "I think she used to be an actress or something."

"Rouge Poisson?" Grandpa says as they leave the desk. "No actress I've ever heard of."

He and the kids walk slowly though the exhibit filled with treasures from many films.

"This stuff is pretty cool," Gum admits as they walk.

"It's my life's work," a woman says. "Hello, Samuel Archer. Don't you recognize me?"

"Jasmine de la Fleur," Grandpa Sam says.

TURN THE PAGE.

He steps up to the woman and takes off his hat. "Then it is you." he adds.

"Of course," she says. "I'm happy to see you."

"You have no idea how happy I am to see you," Grandpa says.

"Ma'am," says Cat, "do you know Rouge Poisson, the curator of the exhibit?"

Jasmine laughs lightly. "I am Rouge Poisson," she says quietly. "That is the name I've used for the last fifty years, ever since I left Hollywood."

"Jasmine," Grandpa says, "I admit I'm surprised to find you here, and working so closely with Sebastian."

"Wait, what?" Sam says, pulling out her notebook. "You know Sebastian?"

Grandpa nods. "I should have told you," he says, "but I didn't want Sebastian to know who I was just yet. It seems he's forgotten me, and if he's the crook—"

"Better to have the advantage on him," Sam finishes.

"You don't mean little Sebby Hammett?" Jasmine says.

"Of course I do," Grandpa says. "He's the projectionist for *The Long Sleep*."

"How can this be?" Jasmine says. "I haven't seen that man in over fifty years."

"Then you didn't know," Grandpa concludes. "I know you two didn't part on good terms."

"Nor you," Jasmine says. "He hated you for sweeping me off my feet and out of his arms."

Jasmine takes Grandpa's hand in hers.

"Ahem," Sam says. "The mystery, Grandpa?"

"Right," Grandpa says. "You've heard about what happened to your film this morning."

"I just spoke to Orlando about it," Jasmine says. "It's the only copy known. If we can't find that section of film . . ."

"Then it wasn't you," Egg says.

"Of course not," Jasmine says. "Why would I do such a thing?"

TURN THE PAGE.

"Then the only suspect we've got left is Sebastian himself," Sam says.

"Is he in the booth right now?" Jasmine asks.

"We left him in the break room thirty minutes ago," Egg says.

"He must be up there now. Let's go," Jasmine says.

Jasmine marches through the door. "They're with me!" she calls to the young man at the info booth as Grandpa and the four young detectives follow her through the door.

"This way," Jasmine says, leading the gang up a set of stairs. At the top is a door marked "Projection Booth."

Jasmine knocks.

"Don't you know," says an angry voice from inside, "you should never disturb a projectionist so close to show time?!"

The door swings open, and there stands Sebastian Hammett. "Oh, Jas—I mean, Rouge," he stammers. "It's you. Is anything wrong?"

"Don't act dumb, Sebby," she says.

The small room is cluttered with equipment, but everything is labeled and stacked carefully on metal shelves. In the center of the room are two projectors, each pointing out a small window toward the screen.

"You remember me," Sebastian says. "Good. Then you'll know—and so you will you, Samuel Archer, my nemesis—why I've edited *The Long Sleep* as I have."

"Then you admit it!" Sam says.

"Of course I admit it," he says. "Both of these cold-hearted lovebirds know who I am. I stole those frames so the world would never see what a great actress Jasmine de la Fleur was, just like I destroyed all the original prints of the film fifty years ago!"

"You lousy weasel!" Grandpa says. "You ended a great acting career!"

"After what she and you did to me?" Sebastian says. "It should have been me with Jasmine at the movie's premiere fifty years ago."

TURN THE PAGE.

"Oh, Sebastian," Jasmine says. "You never did understand what love truly meant."

"Love, shmove," Sebastian says. "I wanted revenge, and I got it. And now that you're both here," Sebastian says, "I will burn the last bit of film ever graced by Jasmine de la Fleur."

He pulls a slim, tan envelope from the pocket of his jacket. He pulls a book of matches from the other.

"Hand it over," Sam says, stepping up to the angry old man. "You have no right!"

"Bah!" Sebastian says. "Don't I deserve justice?"

"That's not justice," says a man's voice. Everyone turns toward the door. It's a man in a jacket and fedora. He flashes a badge. "I'm justice. Drop the matches, Mr. Hammett."

Sebastian drops the matches and the envelope.

"Detective Jones!" Gum says. "From the River City Police Department!"

TURN THE PAGE.

"How did you know to come here?" Sam asks.

The detective smiles as one of his officers places handcuffs on Sebastian. "Your friend Edward called me and kept the phone on this whole time," the detective explains.

"You got here so fast, though," Cat says.

"Well," Detective Jones says, "I happen to be a big fan of film noir. I was already at the exhibit."

"I spotted him downstairs earlier, so I knew he'd come quickly," Egg says.

"Jasmine, I'd love to have you over for supper while you're in town," Grandpa Sam says.

"I'm sure Grandma would love it too," Sam puts in.

Jasmine turns to her. "Don't worry, dear," she says. "I have no intention of stealing away your grandpa."

"Then you're welcome any time, ma'am," Sam says. "Any time at all."

THE END

TO FOLLOW ANOTHER PATH, TURN TO PAGE 20.

"Thanks for helping me with this," Cat says. "I really love that bracelet."

"Of course!" Sam says. "Would we let our favorite animal lover go without her favorite animal-loving bracelet?"

Cat smiles at her. She and her best friends are back in the crowded AR/VR Experience.

Orlando is nowhere to be seen, but a few college-age employees in museum polo shirts and tan pants are there to help.

"I'm still mad that Orlando didn't let us hurry right back in to look," Gum says. "The longer you wait to look, the colder the trail gets."

"Why didn't he let us come right back?" Egg asks.

Cat shrugs. "He probably just wanted to keep the tour moving," she says.

"Hmm," Sam says. She pulls out her notebook and pencil. "I think I know what Egg is getting at."

TURN THE PAGE.

Cat tilts her head. "What do you mean?" she asks.

"What if the bracelet didn't just fall off," Egg says, "but was actually stolen?"

"By Orlando?" Gum says. "That's crazy. Why would he want Cat's animal bracelet?"

"I don't know," Egg says. "It is a silver bracelet, isn't it?"

Cat nods. "Sterling silver," she says.

"So it must be worth something," Sam says. She makes a note in her clues notebook.

"Not as much as it's worth to me, though," Cat says. "It's even engraved."

Egg pats her on the back. "We'll find it," he says. "Let's go check the lost and found. Maybe someone already has."

"Excuse me," Cat says as she steps up to a young woman in a black polo shirt. Her shirt has the logo of the Museum of Moving Pictures. Under that is embroidered the name *Haley*.

"Yes?" the girl says, smiling.

Cat likes her at once, not just because she smiles. She's wearing a gold necklace with a little cat pendant on it with emerald eyes.

"I really like your necklace," Cat tells her.

"Oh, thank you," Haley says. She takes the charm between two fingers and admires it herself. "Do you like animals?"

Cat nods. "In fact," she says, "that's what I wanted to ask you about. I lost a bracelet here this morning."

"An animal bracelet?" Haley says.

"From the zoo," Cat says. "I saved my holiday money and sponsored two seals. The zoo gave me an engraved silver bracelet as a thank-you."

"I'd say we definitely have to get that back for you," Haley says. "Let's start with the lost and found. Do you know where it is?"

Haley pulls out a map of the museum. "Right here is the AR/VR Experience." She points at the map. "Follow this hall to the Special Events and Field Trips Office . . . here!"

TURN THE PAGE.

"Thank you so much," Cat says.

"Just a minute," Gum says, stepping between Cat and Haley.

"Yes?" Haley says.

"You seem in an awful big hurry to get her out of here," Gum says. "Just what are you hiding?"

"Gum!" Cat says. "Don't be rude."

"It's OK," Haley says. "You kids can stay as long as you like. If your bracelet is in the lost and found, it's not going anywhere, after all."

"Thanks," Sam says. She pulls out her notebook and writes a few things down. "Anyone else working the exhibit right now?"

"Sure," Haley says. "Brian . . ." She points toward the AR room, where a young man in a black polo stands outside the door. A red lighted sign above the door reads "SHOW IN PROGRESS."

"Is that light always on when people are inside?" Egg asks.

"Yep, and that's Charlie," Haley adds as she points to the kiosk where guests can pick up VR goggles. One guest is stomping his foot and demanding more time with his goggles.

"Uh-oh," Cat says. "Looks like Charlie's met Anton Gutman."

"I demand an extra five minutes of time," Anton, the class bully, shouted at Charlie, "to make up for the fifteen minutes I was in that dumb AR Experience booth!"

Charlie's face is red as he stammers, "We have a lot, um, a lot of people waiting, and—"

"I don't care about the other people!" Anton screams.

"I better help him out," Haley says. She hands Cat the map. "Here, you can keep this. Good luck finding your bracelet."

"Come on," Sam says. "Let's have a chat with Brian. He seems to be running the AR booth. Maybe he's seen the bracelet."

TURN THE PAGE.

The AR booth sign is lit, but the entrance door is unattended.

"That's weird," Egg says as he and his friends step up to the booth. "Wasn't he here just a second ago?"

Just then, the exit door of the AR Experience opens. Brian comes out.

He is a tall and thin young man. He's wearing a black polo similar to Haley's. His cheeks are red and pocked, and his brown eyes are half closed, like he's either very tired or very bored. Or both.

"You'll have to wait outside a few more minutes," Brian says as the four junior detectives approach the AR booth entrance. "There's a group in there right now."

"We just wanted to ask you something, actually," Egg says.

"Have you been here at the AR booth all morning?" Sam asks.

Brian glances at the watch on his wrist. "I started at nine," he says. "The museum opened at 8:30."

"That's when we got here," Egg says.

"You're on the field trip?" Brian asks.

The kids nod.

"Then Orlando gave you a tour before I was on the clock," Brian says.

"Right," Sam says. "And have you seen Orlando?"

"Not since I first came on," Brian says. "He left a little after nine in a hurry."

Sam makes a note of that. "Anything else seem odd about him?" she asks.

"I wouldn't say being in a hurry is odd exactly," Brian says. "He's in a hurry a lot of the time."

A buzzer sounds.

"Excuse me," Brian says. He opens the exit door of the AR booth, and a group of six people come out.

TURN THE PAGE.

"Thank you. Did you enjoy it?" he asks them as they leave.

It's a group of grown-ups. "Very interesting," says an older woman.

"Lots of fun!" says an older man. He mimes the frost and fire spells.

He's as excited as a little kid. His wife laughs and says, "It's good for him to get out and have fun when he can get a morning off."

Brian laughs. "Have another try later on," he says.

"Six people in one group?" Egg says. "Must be crowded in there. We only had four."

"No way," Brian says. "They never turn the booth on for less than five, even for field trips."

"Huh," Sam says. She makes a quick note in her book.

The group of six adults begins to walk out of the AR/VR exhibit when the older woman stops suddenly. "I've lost my necklace!" she shouts. "Oh, Mortimer. You have to go back in and get it."

Mortimer returns to the entrance. "Young man, please open the door me," he says. "My wife Ethel lost her necklace in there."

"I'm afraid I can't let anyone in once their time is up," he says. "Our staff is inside right now cleaning up and getting ready for the next guests."

"Cleaning up?" Ethel says, aghast. "Do you mean they're in there vacuuming up my necklace?"

"Of course not," Brian says. "But anything they find will go to the lost and found."

"That's what they told me too," Cat says, "after I lost my bracelet this morning."

"Hmm," Ethel says. "Well, I'm going to the lost and found right now."

"We're going there too," Cat says. "We'll walk with you."

Ethel and Mortimer start on their way, but Sam grabs Cat's wrist to stop her.

"Uh-uh," Sam says as she scans her notes. "There's still another worker we haven't questioned."

To question Charlie, turn to page 88.
To go to the lost and found with Ethel, turn to page 94.

"Hi, Charlie," Sam says as the young sleuths step up to the VR booth.

"Um, hi," Charlie says. "Do I know you?"

Cat shakes her head. "We're just hoping you might help us," Cat says. "Well, me, actually. I lost my bracelet."

Charlie nods slowly, as if he's very wise in the ways of missing bracelets. "Happens in this exhibit all the time," he says.

"Really?" Egg says. "Why would that be?"

Charlie glances across the exhibit at Brian by the AR booth. "Some people say it's because everyone moves around a lot," Charlie explains, "so little pieces of jewelry like earrings, bracelets, rings—even necklaces—are bound to get lost sometimes."

"But you don't think so?" Sam asks.

"I think someone on the staff has a good thing going, if you know what I mean," Charlie says. "A little side hustle, if you know what I mean."

"Charlie, this is Sam," Gum says. "Sam, this is Charlie. I think you two are going to get along great."

Charlie makes a confused face. He shrugs.

"Brian thinks Orlando is the culprit," Sam says. "Do you think so too?"

"Pff," Charlie says. "Not a chance. Orlando is the best paid member of the staff."

"And what about you?" Egg asks. "Are you well paid?"

"Well enough," Charlie says. "I live with my parents and spend my free time playing online computer games. My expenses are low."

"So Brian makes about the same?" Cat asks. "And Haley?"

"I guess so," Charlie says. "We have pretty much the same job. Haley lives at home too, but Brian's in college and has an apartment nearby. Can't be cheap, either. I don't know how he affords it."

TURN THE PAGE.

Sam and Egg exchange glances. Cat nods. The three friends look at Gum.

"OK, OK," Gum says. "Even I know this one. Let's go have a little chat with Brian."

***

The young man stands at the entrance to the AR booth. Above him, the red-lighted sign reads "SHOW IN PROGRESS."

"Hi, kids," Brian says. "Ready for another AR experience?"

"Not exactly," Cat says. "We actually wanted to talk to you about the missing jewelry again."

Brian opens his mouth to respond, but Sam cuts him off.

"That's right," Sam says. "It seems you might have a motive to—let's say, *unburden* guests of their valuables."

"What are you talking about?" Brian says. "Just because this twerp lost her bracelet doesn't mean someone stole it, especially not me."

TURN THE PAGE.

"College tuition sure is expensive these days," Gum says. He bounces his eyebrows suggestively.

"Yeah," Brian says, "which is why I have this job, and I don't need a gang of dork babies messing it up for me. Now scram."

"All right," Egg says. "We'll scram, but if we go to Orlando with this tip he might—"

"Oh, wait a second," Brian says, patting the pockets of his pants. "I just remembered. One of the guests found this in the booth."

He pulls a bracelet from his pocket.

"It wouldn't be the one you *lost*, would it?" he says, holding it out in front of Cat like a hypnotist dangling a pocketwatch.

Cat snatches it away. "That *is* my bracelet," she says. "You did steal it!"

"Prove it," Brian says. "Now, run along. I see your *kindergarten* teacher waiting for you in the lobby. I guess your little field trip is over."

"Why you . . . ," Cat says.

"Buh-bye, babies," Brian says.

"You won't get away with this!" Sam says.

But just then, Mr. Spade puts a firm hand on Sam's shoulder and Gum's shoulder. "On the bus, you four," he says.

He smiles at Brian. "Thanks for being such great hosts for my kids today," Mr. Spade says.

"Our pleasure, sir!" Brian says with a big phony grin.

The four friends climb onto the bus.

"At least I have my bracelet," Cat says, admiring it as it dangles on her wrist.

"It's too bad Brian will probably keep stealing, though," Egg says.

"Oh, no way," Sam says. "I'll be back, and his days as a thief are numbered."

THE END

TO FOLLOW ANOTHER PATH, TURN TO PAGE 20.

"What did you lose, dear?" Ethel asks Cat as they walk to the lost and found.

The other adults and Cat's friends hurry ahead, but Ethel moves slowly. Cat stays with her.

"A bracelet," Cat says. "I can't imagine anyone else would even want it but it means a lot to me."

"I know what you mean," Ethel says. "My necklace was a gift from my mother."

"Is it valuable?" Cat asks.

"To me, it's priceless," Ethel says. "To my insurance company . . . well, let's just say if I were to sell it, Mortimer and I could retire quite nicely in Palm Springs."

"Wow," Cat says. "My missing bracelet would probably buy lunch for me and my friends at Luigi's Pizza."

Ethel laughs and takes Cat's arm. "Ah!" she says. "Here's the office."

"Yup," Cat says. She reads the sign aloud: "Special Events and Field Trips."

"Now look here," says an angry voice from inside the open doorway. "We paid good money to have a look around this little funhouse, but enough's enough. I'm not leaving this office until you hand over that necklace!"

"Sounds like Morty got to the office before us," Ethel says. "He should know better. He works so hard and gets so mad. He'll do himself in one of these days."

Cat and she hurry along.

"We're trying to calm him down," Egg says, rushing over to Cat and Ethel. "But he's furious."

"I'll see what I can do," Ethel says. She goes to her husband and speaks quietly to him.

"So," Sam says, leaning close to Cat, "did you pump the old broad for the skinny?"

"Did I what?" Cat says.

"Sam is asking if you questioned Ethel about the possible theft," Egg explains.

"Oh, of course," Cat says. "I should have known."

TURN THE PAGE.

She turns to Sam. "You must be rubbing off on me, Sam," she says, "because I did find out that the missing necklace—a gift from her mother—is worth a lot of money."

"Hmm," Sam says, pulling out her notebook and pencil.

"Oh!" Cat says, "she also said it's insured."

Sam's eyes go wide. "Now we're talkin'."

To accuse the old couple of faking the theft, continue on to page 97.

To ask the people at the lost and found if they have the bracelet, turn to page 100.

"I'll handle this," Sam says as she slips her notebook back into her pocket.

"Please, Sam," Cat says, holding her arm. "Be nice to them. Ethel has been very sweet to me."

"Ethel," Sam says, stepping up to the woman. Sam is a few inches taller than Ethel, but Ethel's manner is graceful and self-assured.

"I was sorry to hear about the missing necklace," Sam says.

"Thank you, sweetie," Ethel says. "You're a friend of Cat's, I assume?"

Sam nods. "I suppose on the bright side," she says, "your husband Mortimer won't have to work anymore."

"Whatever do you mean?" Ethel says.

"You said Mortimer works very hard," Sam says, "I'm surprised he isn't retired yet."

Ethel says nothing.

"Maybe I should speak to Mortimer about it," Sam says.

TURN THE PAGE.

"No, please don't," Ethel says. She puts a gentle hand on Sam's wrist. "I'll come clean."

Sam watches as Ethel goes to her husband.

"Morty," Ethel says. "Let the nice people be. The necklace isn't lost."

"What?" Mortimer says. "You found it?"

"No, no," Ethel says. "I . . . hid it."

"Ettie, I'm confused," Mortimer says.

"I hid it and pretended it had been stolen in that AR contraption," she says.

"Why would you do that?" Mortimer says, but he seems to figure it out and sits on a bench. "Ah. Because I'm a stubborn old fool."

Ethel sits beside him. "You already said you don't want me to sell it," she says. "But without that money, I'm afraid you'll never retire. You need rest, my little meatball."

Mortimer shakes his head. "So you thought you'd sell it secretly instead, eh?" he says.

"You sure cracked that one, Sam," Cat says. "I'm impressed. But what about my bracelet?"

"Next thing on my list," Sam says. "Now, where were we?"

"Time to get back on the bus, kids," Mr. Spade says, poking his head into the lost-and-found office. "Sorry, Cat, but if they don't have your bracelet, you'll have to call them later to see if it turns up."

"Oh, phooey," Cat says. "This isn't how I hoped this mystery would turn out."

"Sorry, kid," Sam says, putting an arm around her shoulders. "I guess the bigger bait caught the fish today."

"Sam," Cat says as they walk out the bus, "I wish I knew what you were talking about."

THE END

To follow another path, turn to page 20.

The four sleuths step up to the lost-and-found counter.

"Hi," Cat says. "I lost my bracelet this morning in the AR Experience booth. Has it shown up here?"

"You're the tenth guest this week to ask about something lost in that booth," says the woman behind the counter.

The woman puts down on the counter a plastic bin full of small trinkets.

"Maybe it's the AR trolls stealing everyone's stuff," the woman says.

"Is it in there?" Egg asks.

Cat shakes her head. "Nothing but single gloves and knit caps and reading glasses," she says.

"I had a feeling we wouldn't find anything here," Sam says. "Something stinks at this museum, and it's not the lost and found. We need to ask some more questions. "

TO QUESTION ORLANDO, TURN TO PAGE 102.
TO QUESTION BRIAN, TURN TO PAGE 106.

The kids find Orlando at the video game exhibit.

"Here for a rematch?" he asks when Gum walks up to him with his friends.

"We didn't finish the first match!" Gum says.

"Actually," Cat says, stepping between them, "remember how I lost my bracelet this morning?"

"But you wouldn't let us go back and look for it?" Gum puts in.

"Yes, I remember," Orlando says. "Did it turn up in lost and found?"

Cat shakes her head. "In fact," she goes on, "the woman at lost and found told us lots of people have been losing stuff in the AR Experience, but none of it turned up."

Orlando shrugs. "It can get pretty chaotic in there. I can see how people, including yourself, might lose a piece of jewelry."

"Then where do they go?" Cat asks. "Why didn't the cleaning crew find it when they were getting ready for the next group?"

"Now that I don't know," Orlando says. "We've talked to the cleanup crew and gone over their equipment. But we found nothing."

"That means someone else had to be in there to pick it up," Egg concludes. "I sure wish I took some photos. Maybe there would have been a clue in them."

"Well, wasn't there someone with us?" Gum asks. "Brian told us that we had to have at least five people to go in, and we only had four."

"That's right!" Cat says. "But I only saw the three of you in there."

"If someone was in there with us, we'd never know, would we?" Sam asks.

"What do you mean?" Cat asks. "We could see each other even with the glasses."

"But everything we saw was changed by the glasses we wore," Sam points out. "It would have been easy for someone else to be in there with us if they knew just where to stand."

"To be hidden by one of the trolls!" Egg says.

TURN THE PAGE.

"Or that ogre," Gum adds. "That thing could've probably hidden a few people."

"There's one way to find out," Egg says. "Didn't you say the gift shop has photos of the experience?"

Orlando nods. "That's right!" he says.

"Let's go," Sam says.

The gift shop is near the exit. "Hi, Orlando," says the man at the counter. "Got a field trip today?"

"Listen, Karl," Orlando says. "Can you bring up the photos of these kids in the AR booth?"

Karl brings up a series of photos on the display of his computer.

"There we go," he says.

"Flip through them," Egg says. "Can we see if anyone is behind the trolls?"

"Let's see . . . ," Karl says. "Ah! Here. Someone is standing right where the ogre appears down the hall. I can't make out who it is."

"Black polo shirt, though," Sam points out. "An employee."

"An employee who hadn't started work yet," Orlando says. "I think I better have a little chat with Brian."

***

"Thank you so much, you guys," Cat says as the four best friends climb back on the bus after their field trip. "I feel bad that Brian got fired, though."

"You feel bad?" Sam says in disbelief. "Cat, some of those people may never get their stuff back."

"That's true," Cat says. She plays with the bracelet on her wrist. "Anyway, we should come back here soon. I think there's a mystery story AR we can try."

Sam waves her off. "Pff," she says. "We don't need any crazy glasses for that. We have real life!"

THE END

TO FOLLOW ANOTHER PATH, TURN TO PAGE 20.

"Hi," Brian says as the four sleuths walk up to him at the AR booth. "Going to try out AR again?"

"Can we ask a few questions?" Egg says.

"Sure," Brian says. "That's what I'm here for."

"The woman in the lost and found gave me an idea," Sam says.

"What idea?" Brian says.

"When she joked that maybe it was the trolls stealing things," Sam says. "I realized it would be easy for someone else to be in there if they knew the image of a troll would block anyone from seeing them."

"What are you getting at?" Brian says. "Unless you have evidence of something—"

"Which is where the gift shop comes in," Cat says, pulling out a photo.

"Right there," Cat says, pointing at a corner of the photo where three trolls are huddled together. "It's a man in a black polo shirt and tan pants."

"It's me," Brian says. "Well, so what? That doesn't prove anything."

"Maybe not on its own," Sam says. "But we can have the gift shop print up a photo of every AR booth visit when a piece of jewelry went missing."

"Then I'll delete all the photos," Brian says through gritted teeth, leaning closer to them. "I work here, so I can do that."

"Correction, Brian," Orlando says, stepping out from his hiding spot. "You worked here. Clean out your locker and return the stolen items."

***

"We did it!" Cat says later as the four friends board the bus. "Thanks, you guys."

"Our pleasure," Sam says. "When it's personal, we always come through."

THE END

TO FOLLOW ANOTHER PATH, TURN TO PAGE 20.

literary news

MYSTERIOUS WRITER REVEALED!

Steve Brezenoff is the author of the Field Trip Mysteries, the Museum Mysteries, and the Ravens Pass series of thrillers, as well as three novels for older readers. Steve lives in Minneapolis, Minnesota, with his wife, Beth, and their two children, Sam and Etta.

arts & entertainment

ARTIST IS KEY TO SOLVING MYSTERY, SAY POLICE

Marcos Calo lives happily in A Coruña, Spain, with his wife, Patricia (who is also an illustrator), and their daughter, Claudia. When Marcos and Patricia aren't drawing, they like to go on long walks by the sea. They also watch a lot of films and eat Nutella™ sandwiches. Yum!

A Detective's Dictionary

amateur – done by people who play for fun, not money

authorize – to give official permission to do something or go somewhere

augmented reality – a kind of technology, such as a video or video game, that puts computer generated images over the real world

virtual reality – realistic 3D world drawn by a computer that can be seen using a special headset

floppy disk – a small, thin piece of flexible plastic coated with magnetic particles used for storing information from a computer

glamorous – attractive and exciting

noir – a kind of film popular in the 1940s and 1950s that usually focused on detectives and crime in big cities

phony – not true or real

rematch – a second game or match between two players or teams

suspenseful – to be filled with worry and unease

FURTHER INVESTIGATIONS

CASE #YCSFTMTMMSI9

1. Orlando, the museum's director, is often absentminded and aloof. Do you think his forgetfulness helps the criminals in the museum with their schemes?

2. Sam is very excited to see the film noir section of the museum. If you visited the Museum of Moving Pictures, which would you be most excited to see and why?

3. No one working at the museum is really sure who the men working on the game machine are. Why do you think the men are able to hide in plain sight?

IN YOUR OWN DETECTIVE'S NOTEBOOK . . .

1. Sam and her grandfather sometimes talk in the style of old detectives. Imagine you are an old detective and write a paragraph in that style.

2. The junior detectives sometimes accuse people who aren't guilty. Write a letter of apology from all four to someone in the book they accused who wasn't guilty.

3. Cat's favorite bracelet is stolen in the augmented reality exhibit. Imagine you are Cat, and write about how you felt when you realized the bracelet was missing, and how you felt when it was found.